The Lord's Prayer

By

Albert Hay Malotte

Brass Quintet

(Score and Parts)

Arranged by John Moss

ED-3982

ISBN 978-0-7935-4085-3

G. SCHIRMER, *Inc.*

DISTRIBUTED BY
HAL•LEONARD® CORPORATION
7777 W. BLUEMOUND RD. P.O. BOX 13819 MILWAUKEE, WI 53213

THE LORD'S PRAYER

Albert Hay Malotte
arranged by John Moss

Adagio, religioso (♩ = ca. 76)

11
mp
mp
mp
mp
15
mf
mf
mf
mf
mf
3
20
mp sub.
mp sub.
mp sub.
mp sub.
mp sub.

24
mp
mp
mp
mp
mf
mp
28
mf
mp
32
mf
f
mf
f
(lead)
mp cresc. poco a poco
mp cresc. poco a poco
mp cresc. poco a poco
mp cresc. poco a poco

THE LORD'S PRAYER

TRUMPET 1 in B♭

Albert Hay Malotte
arranged by John Moss

Adagio, religioso (♩ = ca. 76)

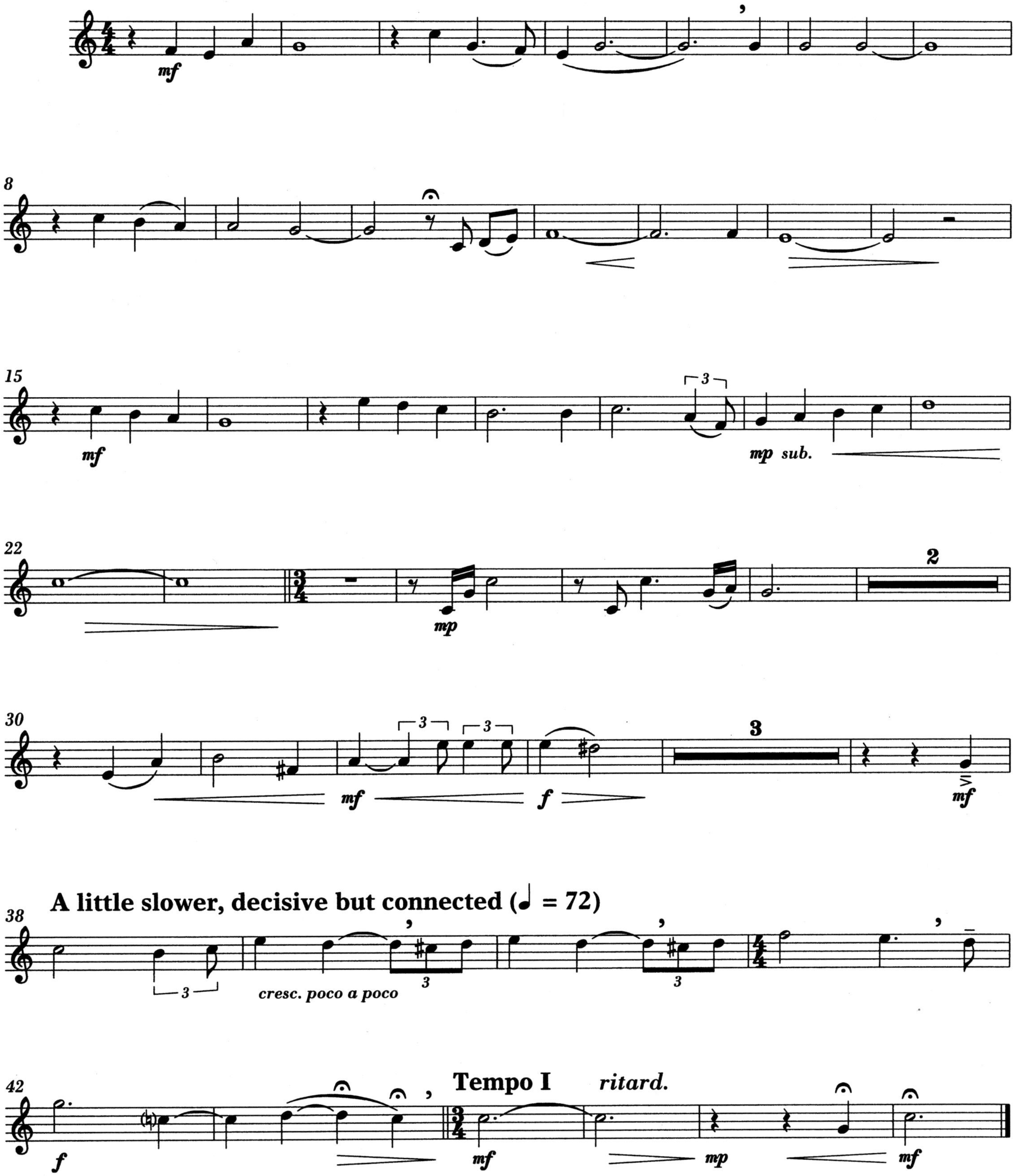

THE LORD'S PRAYER

TRUMPET 2 in B♭

Albert Hay Malotte
arranged by John Moss

THE LORD'S PRAYER

HORN in F

Albert Hay Malotte
arranged by John Moss

THE LORD'S PRAYER

TROMBONE

Albert Hay Malotte
arranged by John Moss

THE LORD'S PRAYER

TUBA

Albert Hay Malotte
arranged by John Moss

A little slower, decisive but connected (♩ = 72)